SCHNITZEL'S FIRST CHRISTMAS

SCHNITZEL'S
FIRST CHRISTMAS

Written and illustrated by Hans Wilhelm

Simon & Schuster Books For Young Readers

Published by Simon & Schuster

New York   London   Toronto   Sydney   Tokyo   Singapore

SIMON & SCHUSTER BOOKS FOR YOUNG READERS, Simon & Schuster Building, Rockefeller Center , 1230 Avenue of the Americas, New York, New York 10020. Copyright © 1989 by Hans Wilhelm
All rights reserved including the right of reproduction in whole or in part in any form.
SIMON & SCHUSTER BOOKS FOR YOUNG READERS
is a trademark of Simon & Schuster
Manufactured in the United States of America.

10 9 8 7 6 5 4 3 2

(pbk) 10 9 8 7 6 5 4 3 2 1

Library of Congress Cataloging-in-Publication Data. Wilhelm, Hans, 1945–   Schnitzel's first Christmas.   Summary: A puppy can't think what he wants for Christmas, but Santa knows just the thing.   [1. Christmas—Fiction.   2. Dogs—Fiction]   I. Title.   PZ7.W64816Sc   1989
[E]   89-5858
ISBN: 0-671-67977-5   ISBN: 0-671-74494-1 (pbk)

To H. H.
for being the friend he is

It was Schnitzel's first winter. He spent his days playing in the fluffy white snow, the first he had ever seen. He would jump up from time to time to catch a snowflake as it fell. On days like this, Schnitzel would come home hungry and exhausted.

But lately, he would have to wait for his supper. And no one seemed to have any time to play with him. What was happening? Why was everyone in such a rush?

He complained to Gruff, the cat.
"Oh," yawned Gruff, "it's Christmas again."
Schnitzel had heard the word Christmas before, and he had heard about someone called Santa Claus, but he really didn't know what all this meant.
"It sounds like Christmas will be a lot of fun," he said, hoping Gruff would tell him more about it.
"It will be if you get a present from Santa Claus," mumbled Gruff.

"Won't Santa bring me one?"
asked Schnitzel, looking worried.

"Only if you wish for one before
he comes on Christmas Eve," said
Gruff.

"Hmm," said Schnitzel. "What
kind of present?"

"Anything you want,"
replied Gruff.

Schnitzel thought for a while. Then he asked Gruff: "Do you have a wish?"

Gruff purred: "Sure, I want a toy mouse. And you?"

"Oh, I'll have to think about it," replied Schnitzel.

"Well, you'd better hurry," Gruff yawned again. "Tonight is Christmas Eve."

"Oh, my," thought Schnitzel. "So little time."
Should he wish for a toy, too? No, he already
had all the toys in the world.

here were always enough
noes and socks lying
round for him to chew on.

There were always so many
things in the children's
room to play with.

And there was always a
squirrel who asked to
be chased.

No, he didn't need another toy.

Perhaps there was something else he could wish for. He wondered if Humber, the goldfish, could help him.

"Do you have a Christmas wish?" he asked Humber.

"Of course I do!" bubbled Humber. "I want a beautiful water castle to sleep in. That's my wish."

"Perhaps I should wish for a new place to sleep, too," thought Schnitzel.

"Do you have a Christmas wish?" he asked a sparrow.

"Yes," she chirped. "I want to have plenty of food: some nice seeds and tasty kernels, and perhaps some yummy raisin bread crumbs. In winter, there's nothing more important than food for us birds. Believe me!"

"Maybe I should wish for some food, too," thought Schnitzel.

If only there were someone who understood what a little puppy might wish for! Suddenly he felt very lonely.

"I'll just have to keep asking," thought Schnitzel, and went outside.

But he already had the most comfortable, warm, soft blanket and cushion any dog might ask for!

"But I already have all the dog food and treats
any puppy might want!"

It seemed he had everything he could wish for—except a Christmas wish!

Gruff opened one eye. "Have you made your wish yet?" he asked.

"Oh, yes," fibbed Schnitzel, not wanting to look foolish.

"Well, what is it?" demanded Gruff.

"It's a secret!" replied Schnitzel.

He felt awful.

That evening, the house was full of excitement. Everyone
was running about, and there were boxes, papers and ribbons
all over the place. But Schnitzel felt like hiding.
    "I'm not so sure I like Christmas," he sighed. "No one has any
time for me and no one can help me find a Christmas wish."

That night, Schnitzel went to bed feeling very sad indeed.
He imagined Gruff laughing at him when he didn't get a
present on Christmas morning. It was all too much for a little
puppy.

Schnitzel fell asleep feeling very lonely.

In the middle of the night, Schnitzel was awakened by strange noises.

"There must be a stranger in the house," he thought. "I'd better go and see."

Someone was coming down the chimney. At first, Schnitzel thought it might be a burglar. Then he remembered.

"It must be Santa Claus," he thought, "bringing presents for everyone—except me!"

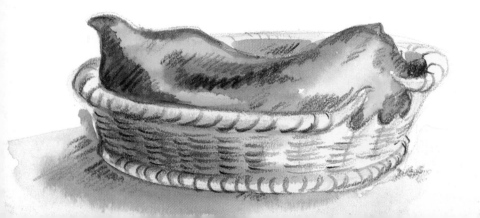

Schnitzel watched Santa Claus putting presents under the tree. When he had finished, he noticed Schnitzel.

"And what's your name, my little friend?" he asked.

"I....I'm Schnitzel," replied Schnitzel.

"Schnitzel? I don't think that name is in my big book. Didn't you make a wish, Schnitzel?" asked Santa.

"I....I couldn't think of anything to wish for," said Schnitzel, feeling a little embarrassed.

"Ho, ho, ho!" laughed Santa Claus. "In all the time I've been around, I can't remember anyone who didn't have a wish. Now let me have a look. Perhaps I have something for you anyway."

Santa opened his bag once more, and searched among all the presents that were left.

"Aha!" he said after a while. "I knew there must be something here that would be just perfect for a little dog who has everything!"

Santa set down a beautifully wrapped present, tied with a bright ribbon.

"This is for you, Schnitzel," he said with a smile.

"For me? A present?" Schnitzel was so surprised and pleased, he could hardly speak.

"Yes, Schnitzel, a special present for you," said Santa. "Now I have lots more gifts to deliver, so I'll say goodbye until next Christmas."

And with that, he was up the chimney and gone.

Schnitzel was so excited, he couldn't wait.

"Wake up everyone!" he cried. "I got a present! Santa was here and I got a present! Come and see!"

Schnitzel danced around his present, pulling on the ribbon to open it.

What *could* be inside?

What a wonderful surprise!

"Merry Christmas," said the little puppy. "I'm Pretzel. And who are you?"

"I...uh...I'm Schnitzel," replied Schnitzel, not quite believing his eyes and ears.

"I like that name," said Pretzel. "Do you like to play?"

"Of course I do!" answered Schnitzel.

"Then let's see if you can catch me!" teased Pretzel.

"O.K." laughed Schnitzel, and off they ran around the Christmas tree, as happy as only two happy puppies can be.

Schnitzel would always remember that first Christmas, when he met his best friend.

And isn't that the best Christmas present anyone could wish for?